THIS

# SPOOKTACULAR

BOOK BELONGS TO

........................................................

........................................................

........................................................

This edition published by Parragon Books Ltd in 2014 and distributed by:

Parragon Inc.
440 Park Avenue South, 13th Floor
New York, NY 10016
www.parragon.com

MONSTER HIGH and associated trademarks and trade dress are

www.monsterhigh.com

ISBN 978-1-4723-6058-8

Printed in China

# CONTENTS

## A MONSTROUS WELCOME

Welcome to Monster High! Come in and pull up a chair. May I start by congratulating you on your choice of school—as you can see, we are quite literally head and shoulders above all the other institutions. Not only does our faculty contain some of the world's most monstrous minds, but our facilities, from our state-of-the-art grimnasium to our new vampitheater, are also second to none. No wonder our OfDead rating is so spooktacular!

I am putting you in the capable (and removable) hands of one of our newest and most fiendly student bodies, Miss Frankie Stein. Frankie will give you a guided tour of the school. You'll get your scary bearings in no time! Over to you Miss Stein . . .

Hey, ghoulfriend, I'm Frankie Stein. It's gruesome starting a new school, but don't freak out. I'm a newbie myself and my first week here was pretty much one huge voltageous fail! Luckily, the beast thing about Monster High is that fitting in is soooo out! I soon got the fang of un-life here and now everyone loves high-voltage me—even though I do have a ghastly habit of accidentally electrocuting the class!

Paste your photos here!

Paste your photos here!

This locker belongs to: ..........................

..........................................................

Age: ..................................................

Pet on the premises: .........................

..........................................................

Ghoul info: .........................................

..........................................................

..........................................................

..........................................................

We're going to start our school tour in the Coffin Corridor. Our coffin lockers are where we store everything, from killer heels to our Fierce 'n' Flawless ma-scarer . . . and the odd Mad Science textbook, of course.

Your locker's right here. Make it ughsomely unique by adding your own deadly details and decor. When you're done, we'll sneak a spooky peak inside the coffins of some of the student bodies, starting with the most freaktacular vampire at Monster High—Draculaura.

# Draculaura ™

**Age:** 1,600 years

**Pet on the premises:**
Count Fabulous™, bat

## Ghoul info:

So the first thing to know about me is that I'm strictly vegetarian. You won't catch me chowing down on raw steak in the creepateria—or more importantly on my fellow student bodies!

I love creative writing and hate ge-ogre-phy—after 1,600 years I've pretty much seen most places (Monster High still comes out on top, I mean, what's not to like?).

What else? Oh, yeah, my signature style. It can be summed up in one word: pink! Baby pink, hot pink, cerise, coral, salmon, fuchsia . . . so many shades and, in my case, soooo much time to wear them all!

My GFFs

I heart Claud Wolf

The cutest bat in the bell tower!

# Clawdeen Wolf™

**Age:** 15 years

**Pet on the premises:**
Crescent™, cat

**Ghoul info:**
If you are reading this then you're snooping in my locker! You're lucky it's not a full moon, because I get more than a little kerrazzy on those nights. Soooo here's the wolfie low-down on the leader of the pack!

I always look fur-rociously fabulous, from my bling-ringed ears all the way down to my paw-fectly manicured claws. Don't let my ughsome style fool you, however—I'm no pushover! I'm loyal, outspoken, and freakily fierce.

Betcha didn't know that I'm also the fastest ghoul in school? I beat Clawd on the track time and again, even in sky-high wedge sneakers!

Family fur-ever!

Ghouls' night out!

# Frankie Stein™

**Age:** How many days is it now?

**Pet on the premises:** Watzit™, puppy

**Ghoul info:**
Hey there, I know what you're thinking—my locker's as messy as a banshee's bathroom! Don't blame me, a ghoul's gotta make sure she has everything she needs to look voltageous at all times. Who knows when I'm going to need to grab an extra neck bolt or recharge?

I guess the best thing about my coffin is that it's right next to Draculaura's and Clawdeen's. That means I get to fang out between classes with my GFFs! It almost makes up for having to endure double math period with Mr. Mummy twice a week. I may only be days old, but I'm dead-termined to enjoy every minute of un-life at Monster High!

Go, Fear Squad!

Cool ghouls!

FEAR SQUAD

Frankie,

Fearleading practice is at midnight. Be there or be scared!

Cleo x

# CLEO DE NILE™

**Age:** (about) 5,842 years

**Pet on the premises:**
Hissette™, Egyptian cobra

**Ghoul info:**
Oh. My. Ra! It's blacker than Khaba's crypt in this coffin. I hate the dark, but if you tell a soul I'll unleash the terrifying power of one of my father's cursed idols on you!

Where to start with my scary-coolness? I'm captain of the fearleading squad, as well as being the most stylish and popular student in the history of Monster High. My sister, Nefera de Nile™, might try to claim otherwise, but don't listen to her—she's more sly than Hissette, my pet cobra!

More about me? Well, my favorite colors are gold and turquoise and I practically live at the maul! The way I see it, a ghoul can never own too many Ghostier bandages.

Me (oh and Ghoulia, too)

With my fave monster

2: Deuce

CDN4DG

# Ghoulia Yelps™

**Age:** 16 years

**Pet on the premises:**
Sir Hoots A Lot™, owl

**Ghoul info:**
Some people might call me an ogre-achiever, but I feel very privileged to be a student at Monster High! I intend to make the most of every opportunity to expand my knowledge and fill my monstrously able mind. I enjoy every subject on the scare-iculum—even dodgeball teaches one to duck. After class, my fave activities include chess and Comic Book Club (of which I am president).

If you need to find me, check out my slime-table. I work to a rigid schedule. If I'm not in class your best bet is the study howl or the libury. Occasionally I fang out at the Coffin Bean with Cleo — they do a fabulous spookaccino!

Cleo's so creeperific!

Ghoulia
DEADFAST

## Lagoona Blue™

**Age:** 15

**Pet on the premises:**
Neptuna™, piranha

**Ghoul info:**
As daughter of the Sea Monster, I'm what at Monster High we call a "salty." My ugh-mazing swim buddy Gil Webber™ is one of the "freshies," which means he's from freshwater stock.

You won't be shocked to hear that I'm the captain of the Monster High swim team. I'm always happiest in the school pool even though the chlorine does dry out my scales and turn my hair blue. It's kind of a scary-cool look though — my GFFs wouldn't have me any other way.

I often store my bag in my coffin locker, but don't dip your fingers in—it's really a fishbowl that I use to smuggle my pet piranha into class!

Gil Webber. Water guy!

Ghoul and the gar

Neptuna's my anti-bag-theft device!

# Abbey Bominable™

**Age:** 16

**Pet on the premises:**
Shiver™, woolly mammoth

**Ghoul info:**
Please excuses for mistakes of spelling—
we do not do much of the writing in
mountains where I am from. It is so
cold there, ink freezes before hits page.

Scary-cool
ghoulfriends

My father, the Yeti, send me
to Monster High. I am living
here at the school—guess you
could call me a "snowboarder!"
Look, I make joke! Is funny, no?

Was difficult at first to be making of the
friends. Back home talking is wasting
oxygen so am not used to doing the
chitchat. Monsters call me rude.
But now they understand that although
my ice-crystal necklace means I am
always cold to the touching, my heart
is not frozen. My GFFs are Frankie
and Lagoona. I like when creepateria
serve cheese of yak on toast.

Boarding is maxed
out totally!

13

Now you see me..

**Age:** 16

**Pet on the premises:**
Rhuen™, ghost ferret

**Ghoul info:**
Psst! Spectra here. I'm the go-to ghoul for info on all the comings and groanings at Monster High. Not a roar or rattle of chains escapes my ghostly gaze. I keep everyone updated through the posts on my blog. Every time I have an eek-citing piece of news to share, it pings up as an alert on the student bodies' iCoffins!

I'm dying to be a journalist when I leave school. Right now I'm cutting my teeth as the dead-itor of the Monster High newspaper. Out of class, if I'm not haunting the bell tower, I can be found eating angel cake in the creepateria. It's light and sweet, just like me!

Rhuen,
My little thief!

*The* **Monster High Mail**

# Rochelle Goyle™

**Age:** 415

**Pet on the premises:**
Roux™, gargoyle griffin

**Ghoul info:**
Hi, *c'est moi*, Rochelle. I come from Scaris and am also . . . how you say . . . ze new ghoul at school. I am very interested in fashion. My own style is a mix of stained glass and wrought iron. Is very classy, *non*? I like to zink zat my look is "timeless." After all, I have been working it for centuries.

My favorite subject at Monster High is architecture— I've spent a lot of time sitting on buildings. *Et* ze subject I detest? Swimming! I'm ze only monster less likely to be in ze pool zan Frankie Stein. If I jumped in I'd sink like a stone.

Zis ghoul is scary-smart!

Moi avec Robecca

# Venus McFlytrap™

**Saving the monster world!**

**Age:** 15

**Pet on the premises:**
Chewlian™, Venus flytrap plant

**Ghoul info:**
Hi there, I'm Venus—bright, loud, and in your face! There's no point in being a wallflower, especially when you've got an important message to deliver to your monster peers. I'm passionate about protecting the environment. I've been tempted to use my pollens of persuasion to get monsters to take care of the Earth, but the effects are only temporary. I've found that talking about it helps to get to the root of the problem! Trashing the planet is so uncool!

I'm a fiendishly friendly type (unless I find out that you're a litterbug) and I love entwining my tendrils with like-minded monsters. Lagoona and Gil totally get the green Venus vibe.

**LET'S GO GREEN**

With my fab GFF!

# Robecca Steam™

**Age:** 116

**Pet on the premises:**
Captain Penny™, mechanical penguin

## Ghoul info:

I used to think of myself as an old-fashioned ghoul, but since coming to Monster High, I have been told that my style is totally "steam punk!"

You might have noticed my rocket boots—they take me anywhere I want to go at top speed. I can even do stunts! I guess I inherited my scaredevil genes from my dad, a mad scientist who is rumored to be lost in the catacombs under the school. Perhaps that is why Monster High always feels like home.

My GFF here is Frankie Stein—we have got so much in common, both having been created by our parents!

With my fab GFF!

# Jinafire Long

**Age:** 15 hundred scales

**Pet on the premises:**
None yet!

**Ghoul info:**
This is the second coffin locker I've had actually—I melted the first. I'm hot-tempered and have a tendency to set fire to things when I get upset.

My style is traditional Asian with a fiercely modern twist. Chinese dragons live for hundreds of years, so I've had a long time to perfect my look. My GFFs are Clawdeen and Skelita Calaveras—we bonded over our love of fashion! Clawdeen has been ugh-mazingly kind, helping me find haunt couture pieces that accommodate my long tail.

My favorite subject is metallurgy. My least favorite? Physical deaducation! Sweat ruins my makeup and makes my scales itch!

Looking fierce with Clawdeen!

The boys from metalwork class

# Skelita Calaveras ™

**Age:** 15

**Pet on the premises:**
None

**Ghoul info:**
*Hola!* Skelita here. This is my locker.
Excuse the crazy sugar skulls—
I've been cooking up batches so my
GFFs Clawdeen and Jinafire can
decorate them. Sugar skulls are
an important part of my scare-itage.
I come from Hexico. Every November
we all celebrate *Día de los Muertos.*
It's such a creepy-colorful fiesta—
you're gonna love it!

In case you're wondering where my pet is,
I'd better explain. I keep millions
of monarch *mariposas* (butterflies).
Sadly they don't like to be contained
in classrooms. I have to wait until I go
back home each winter to enjoy their
fluttery beauty.

Creeptastically
colorful!

# My SPOOKY Scare-itage

This is Mr. Rotter's classroom. Check out the "My Spooky Scare-itage" project his students are working on. Fang-scinating stuff! Some of the ghouls haven't quite finished. Shall we lend them a claw?

Be a good ghoulfriend and help the students complete their assignments on time. Read each piece of work, then fill in the missing words on the dotted lines. The words you need are jumbled up on the green panel!

## My Spooky Scare-itage

NAME: Skelita .................................

DEAD-SCENDED FROM: Los Eskeletos

SCARY-COOL COUNTRY: .................................

MY SCARE-ITAGE: I am very proud of my scare-itage and its legends and traditions. My favorite custom is Día de los ........................... (or Day of the Dead), where we honor our ancestors. We spend time with la familia, hold parties, and decorate our homes with marigold flowers and screamily scrummy sugar skulls.

## MY SPOOKY SCARE-ITAGE

NAME: ......................... Long

DEAD-SCENDED FROM: Chinese .................................

SCARY-COOL COUNTRY: China

MY SCARE-ITAGE: The country of my fore-monsters is very eek-xotic with customs and traditions that have carried on for thousands and thousands of years. Monsters like me were often found guarding temples. We have always had great powers and can control elements including ...................., wind, and water.

# MY SPOOKY SCARE-ITAGE

NAME: Cleo ....... Nile

DEAD-SCENDED FROM: ..............................

SCARY-COOL COUNTRY: .............................

MY SCARE-ITAGE: My father tells me that, traditionally, monsters like me were entombed in pyramids in the middle of the desert with .................... and gold and so much bling. We still live in my father's pyramid and I have my own totes amazing crypt! Our bodies are wrapped in an OTT amount of bandages—which we can never take off!

## MY SPOOKY SCARE-ITAGE

NAME: ..............................

DEAD-SCENDED FROM: The Gargoyles

SCARY-COOL CITY: ..............................

MY SCARE-ITAGE: Stone is a big part of my culture. My ancestors have always been found on and around great ..................., such as castles and cathedrals, which we protect. Although I come from Scaris, monsters like me are found in many countries, including ancient Egypt and Greece. We can take many forms.

THE MUMMY    SCARIS    HEXICO    JINAFIRE    FIRE

DRAGONS    DE    MUERTOS    CALAVERAS

BUILDINGS    JEWELS    ROCHELLE    EGYPT    GOYLE

Complete your own assignment here!

## MY SPOOKY SCARE-ITAGE

NAME: ..............................

DEAD-SCENDED FROM: ..............................

SCARY-COOL COUNTRY: ..............................

MY SCARE-ITAGE: ..............................

..............................

..............................

..............................

# Voltage Vampitheater

Mr. Where's drama class takes place here, in the vampitheater. He has been named as *Stage and Scream Magazine's* "Deadliest Drama King" three years in a row!

Clawdeen has landed the top role in the school production of *A Monster for All Seasons*. She and Cleo de Nile always have their claws out over the leading roles!

It's time for Clawdeen's costume fitting. Design a spooktacular outfit for her to wear. This star won't go on stage looking anything less than ugh-mazing!

# Li-terror-ture

I love this class! Don't you just adore the classics such as Scram Screamer's *Dracula* and, my personal favorite, *Freakenstein,* by Scary Shelley? The professor's away today so the substitute creature Mr. Lou Zarr (snicker) has asked the class to write poetry about the monster sitting next to them.

Oh my ghoul! Who are these mischievous monsters describing? Maybe you can guess . . . Read the odorous odes out loud, then write in the titles.

**1**

.................

by Abbey Bominable

He's a loud-mouthed flirt,
He's kind of lame,
He gets uptight,
Then bursts in flame!
The End

**2**

.................

by Jackson Jekyll™

HER GHOULISH GAZE, EYES BLUE AND GREEN,
SPARKS THAT SPIT FROM EVERY SEAM,
OH, IF SHE COULD ONLY SEE
HOW MUCH SHE MEANS TO "NORMIE" ME.
SHE'S HELPED ME AND MY EGO "HOLT,"
WITH EVERY AMP AND EVERY VOLT
OF HER SPOOKTASTIC MONSTER SELF,
BUT I'M STILL SITTING ON THE SHELF.

**3**

.................

by Operetta™

Oh, whatta ghoul,
This chick's so cool,
The greenest monster
In our school,
Li'l Lagoona is her pal—
Guess she digs this caring gal.

**4**

.................

by Draculaura
He's a hunky casketball star,
And I know he's gonna go far.
Even though his favorite treat,
Is pizza topped with meat,
He's still my favorite guy—
The heart never lies!

# Sweet Meow-sic

This is the music room. Some monsters are really musically talented—like Operetta (although she never sings live for fear of making monsters lose their minds) and the purrfect pop star Catty Noir™. She's so creeperifically cool! We can't believe someone so talon-ted is going to our school. Draculaura and I had a blast at her last concert. It was spooktacular!

Use your pens to fill the stage with Frankie and all her GFFs, rocking out to Ms. Noir's fabulous werecat beat!

# HOME ICk HOMEWORK

Here we are in home ick! Ms. Kindergrübber gives me pretty good grades—I think she was impressed when I baked a life-sized gingerbread man and brought him to life! Today she wants us to think up recipes that celebrate our ughsome individuality. Mine is a high-voltage energy drink. Wanna try it?

## Frankie Stein's joltin' juice

This intensely green smoothie is great at creep-fast time. It tastes super fruity and the energy jolt will really set you up for school!

### For two smoothies, you will need:
- 1 banana, cut into slices
- ½ apple or pear, cored and chopped
- 1½ cups seedless green grapes
- 1½ cups fresh spinach leaves, torn
- 1 cup vanilla yogurt
- Ice cubes to serve

**1.** Place all of the ingredients into a blender or food processor.

**2.** Put the lid on and blend until smooth.

**3.** Fill tall glasses with ice cubes, then pour in the juice.

**4.** Let the smoothies chill for a few minutes. Enjoy!

Always ask an adult before using sharp knives and blenders. Kitchen gadgets can be dangerous!

# GPA QUIZ

## (Ghastly Point Average)

At Monster High we're expected to achieve eek-cellence—we get tested every semester! How much do you know about the monster world? Check your ghastly point average with this fiendishly difficult Scary Aptitude Test.

Are you as scarily smart as Ghoulia Yelps? It's time to put your monstrous mind to the test. Grab a pen and get scribbling!

**1.** The practice of chanting and performing freaky dance moves to support a team is called . . .

A. sport-spooking ☐
B. fearleading ☐
C. rollermazing ☐

**2.** Name a sport played with a ball and a hoop, commonly practiced by monsters at Monster High.

...........................................................

**3.** Unscramble the letters to reveal Ms. Kindergrübber's ghastly subject.

O H E M  K I C

_ _ _ _  _ _ _

**4.** Which of these could cause problems for members of the Monster High swim team?

A. Having Frankie Stein on the team ☐
B. A creature lurking in the deep end ☐
C. Rochelle Goyle diving in the pool ☐

**5.** At the annual Mad Science Fair, student bodies exhibit work that they've invented during which teacher's class?

...........................................................

**6.** Which teacher at Monster High famously does not give As?

...........................................................

**7.** What are the series of dark caves and caverns beneath the school known as?

...........................................................

**8.** When not in class, where should student bodies store their possessions?

..............................................................

**9.** Pets are not allowed in the classrooms.

True ☐
False ☐

**10.** Who at Monster High beat both Mr. Rotter and Mr. Hackington to scoop the coveted Creature of the Year Award?

..............................................................

**11.** Which two dates in the diary add up to the worst bad-luck day ever?

A. Friday the 13th and Valentine's Day ☐
B. Halloween and The Day of the Dead ☐
C. Friday the 13th and October 31st ☐

**12.** Failing a test or getting a very low grade can mean your parents are called in for a . . .

A. parent-creature conference ☐
B. reaper's report ☐
C. Bloodgood bashing ☐

**13.** Which of these is NOT an extra-scare-icular activity at Monster High?

A. Fashion Entrepreneurs' Club ☐
B. Comic Book Club ☐
C. Scream Team ☐

*So . . . how do you measure up?*

Answers on page 69

**0-5**
Uh-oh! You're not eek-actly head ghoul—this monster must try harder.

You know some of your haunting homework, but you'd need to bone up on a few more freaky facts before you're at the top of the class.

**11-13**
Bone-a-fide! With that Ghastly Point Average, you could even give Ghoulia the shivers!

89

# The Paw-fect

I am suggesting that all student bodies find a study buddy with whom to exchange knowledge. Try my logical and geometrical diagram to help you find the pawfect partner with whom to work. Good luck.

Who's your ultimate homework fiend? Answer each question, then follow the arrows to find your scarylicious study buddy.

My pencil case is always freaky-fabulous!

YES

YES

NO

NO

NO

Of course I'll study . . . after fearleading!

YES

YES

Hiss-tory is the best subject on the scare-iculum.

NO

YES

## Frankie Stein

Freaky-fab minds think alike and Frankie is one enthusiastic study buddy! When you've finished comparing scary-cool stationery, you'll get straight down to work on your hiss-tory or home ick assignments.

## Cleo de Nile

Your working partnership with Cleo is sure to be golden. You'd both rather be fearleading than studying, but you'll happily bone up on geometry over a spookaccino at the Coffin Bean!

## Draculaura

Even books need makeovers sometimes, and like Draculaura you spend almost as much time on presentation as content, covering textbooks in fierce paper and highlighting passages in hot-pink pen.

# Study Buddy

START

Learning is much fiercer with a study buddy.

**YES** / **NO**

I'd rather study at the Coffin Bean.

The libury is the beast place to work!

I love scary-cool highlighter pens in ice-blue or pink.

**YES** / **NO**

I'd just die if my grades slipped!

**YES** / **NO**

Talking work through with ghoulfriends helps me study.

When it comes to learning, I'm a high-tech kinda ghoul.

**YES** / **NO**

**NO**

**YES**

**NO**

## bbey Bominable

ou and Abbey are ghouls of few ords, preferring to read and write ather than discuss and recite ssons. You are both logical reatures who shine at math and are t the top of Mr. Mummy's class.

## Ghoula Yelps

An ogre-achiever like you should definitely buddy up with Ghoulia. Just like the clever zombie, you're happiest reading tomes in the libury or researching your next assignment on Boo-gle.

## Robecca Steam

You like to work the traditional way and would rather hand write homework with a quill than use a computer. This is long-winded, but as Robecca always says, "less monster haste— more spooky speed!"

# UN-FEELING CONUNDRUM

There are always lots of comings and groanings in the catacombs beneath the school. Most guys and ghouls come here at some point in the term to see Mr. D'eath, the student body counselor.

Mr. D'eath helps with issues—he's a bony shoulder to cry on! Read each piece of advice, then draw a line to match it to the student who needs it.

**1.** You have had more dead-tentions than you've had nose rings! In a school where we embrace all freaky flaws, there are rumors of you bullying other student bodies. We need to look at anger management sessions.

**2.** You are doing well in the face of extreme prejudice—you should be proud of sticking up for yourself and for your inter-monster relationship. Try to concentrate on your goals and achievements in the pool.

**3.** While it's creeptastic to have strong beliefs, you must understand that not everyone will share your convictions. Tying litterbugs up with tendrils or bewitching them with your pollens is not the answer.

**4.** I'm afraid we cannot sanction skipping school during parts of the lunar cycle. Don't hide in the shadows when the moon is full—continue to be your fabulous self!

A. CLAWDEEN WOLF

B. MANNY TAUR™

C. LAGOONA BLUE

D. VENUS MCFLYTRAP

**Answers on page 69**

# Zombie Super-Highway

Toralei can't understand how I manage to get to all my classes on time, given that zombies move at the speed of the un-dead. Proving that it's better to be scary-smart than freaky-fast, I've created a zombie superhighway in the catacombs. With just a tickle of a dragon's nostril, zombies like me can be sneezed at high speed from one end of the school to the other!

Help Ghoulia fly through the catacombs to attend Mr. Hackington's mad science lesson. Find a pen or pencil, then draw a line all the way to class.

**START**

**FINISH**

Answer on page 69

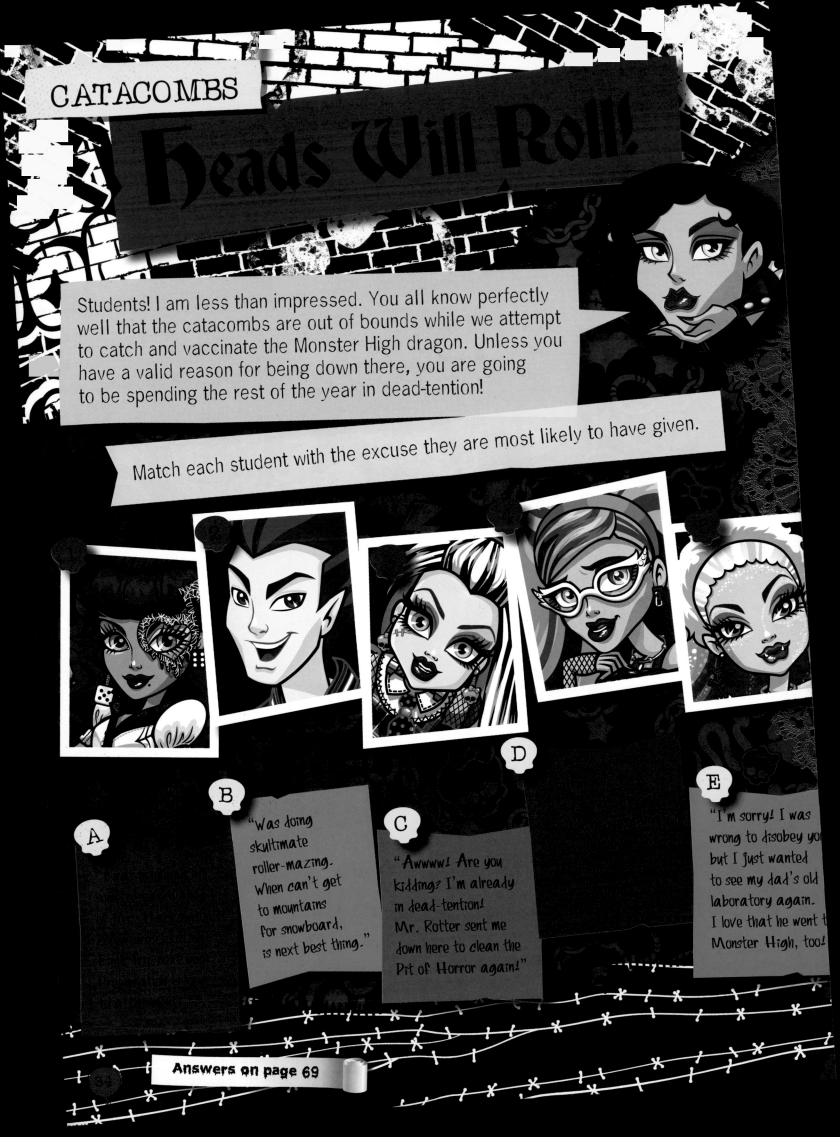

# Heads Will Roll!

Students! I am less than impressed. You all know perfectly well that the catacombs are out of bounds while we attempt to catch and vaccinate the Monster High dragon. Unless you have a valid reason for being down there, you are going to be spending the rest of the year in dead-tention!

Match each student with the excuse they are most likely to have given.

**A**

**B**
"Was doing skultimate roller-mazing. When can't get to mountains for snowboard, is next best thing."

**C**
"Awwww! Are you kidding? I'm already in dead-tention! Mr. Rotter sent me down here to clean the Pit of Horror again!"

**D**

**E**
"I'm sorry! I was wrong to disobey yo but I just wanted to see my dad's old laboratory again. I love that he went t Monster High, too!

Answers on page 69

# WHO'S HIDI... IN THE 'COMBS?

Study the shadows, then write the correct name underneath each fiend. Don't freak if you get stuck—the names are printed at the bottom of the page to help you.

> I spend a lot of time in the catacombs. First, I am always looking out for my dad, who was last seen in these dark caverns. Second, it is a great place to practice stunts in my rocket boots. The catacombs are busy today and some prankster has snuffed out the flaming torches. Can you help me work out who is who?

1.

2.

3.

4.

5.

6.

7.

8.

Answers on page 69

JINAFIRE LONG

ABBEY BOMINABLE

TORALEI STRIPE

CLAWD WOLF

VENUS MCFLYTRAP

...U..E

SKELITA C...L...VERAS

DRACUL..URA

35

# FREAKY PHOTO BOARD

Welcome to the student lounge. We fang out here after school and between classes. You might catch us playing terror-tennis or chillaxing with the back issues of *Teen Scream*. Check out our photo board—it's freaky-fab!

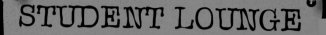

# HELPING HANDS

At Monster High, the student bodies pride ourselves on always lending a hand—literally, in my case—to a fiend in need. We'd do anything for our boos! Here are some examples of the totally voltage ways we've been there for each other.

Invisi Billy helped stone-footed Rochelle Goyle land a part as the lead dancer in Mr. Where's recital. He lifted her in the air to make it look as if she were leaping gracefully!

I helped calm Ghoulia's nerves by offering to be her wing-ghoul for her first date with Slo Mo.

Operetta was glad to help Deuce write a love song for Cleo.

Jinafire helped Deuce, Jackson, Manny, and Heath get their casketball back from a well in the dungeons—and helped them understand that problems can't always be solved by brute force.

I helped the poor zombies get a voice in school by standing up for Slo Mo. I even got him elected Student Disembodied President!

The ghouls all helped Draculaura get to Cleo's big party when she came down with a bad case of polka-dot fever. They made the party polka-dot themed!

Clawdeen, Cleo, and I helped Lagoona out when she was worried about her parent-creature conference.

Scarah Screams helped rewire the buttons and wool inside HooDude's brain to make him feel freaky-fabulous about himself.

Cleo tried her best to help Operetta become more elegant with charm school lessons, before they realized that what counts is being true to your monstrous self.

Use this space to write about all the times you and your GFFs have been there for each other.

My wing-ghoul ............................................................
totally saved my un-life when .............................................
..........................................................................
..........................................................................
..........................................................................
..........................................................................

I'll never fur-get ........................................................
..........................................................................
..........................................................................
..........................................................................

It was really ugh-some when ..............................................
..........................................................................
..........................................................................
..........................................................................

I had to lend a claw to ...................................................

# BATHING BLUE-TY

Here we have the school pool. I'm not in here that much—electricity and water are not a good mix! I was forced to take a dip on the day I dropped Draculaura's fave necklace into the water by mistake. I had to swim down to get it back from the huge creature that lurks in the pool's dark caverns.

Lagoona's a monster you'd totally catch in the pool! She's aquatically ugh-mazing! Use your fave pens or pencils to add some fin-tastic new designs to her swimwear.

40

# WATERY WORDSEARCH

Dip a webbed toe into the watery world of Lagoona Blue. Her scare-itage as the "salty" daughter of the Sea Monster means there's nobody faster or fiercer to captain the Monster High Swim Team to championship victory. The grid below contains 12 words that are always on the tip of Lagoona's tongue. Check them off the list as you find them. Remember, they could be lurking in any direction—horizontally, vertically, or diagonally!

| S | M | I | W | S | I | M | I | N | G | U | O |
|---|---|---|---|---|---|---|---|---|---|---|---|
| A | N | T | E | N | I | R | O | L | H | C | L |
| L | P | R | E | T | A | W | H | S | E | R | F |
| T | T | O | T | V | A | N | O | A | P | J | S |
| W | U | S | U | S | E | A | N | S | R | F | W |
| A | W | E | L | N | B | O | H | S | I | F | F |
| T | C | V | E | L | G | E | T | U | N | E | I |
| E | L | A | V | R | I | T | I | S | D | R | N |
| R | O | W | A | G | O | G | D | I | U | A | S |
| S | R | P | S | E | V | W | E | T | E | R | E |
| R | H | S | N | E | P | T | U | N | E | G | F |
| Y | S | A | E | D | M | J | V | T | N | G | I |

## Final Stroke!

Can you find the extra, 13th word hiding in the grid? It's the chemical that makes Lagoona's scales dry out—and the reason she has to slap on tombs of monsturizer!

_ _ _ _ _ _ _ _

**SEA**          **NEPTUNE**          **GILLS**

**OCEANOGRAPHY**          **SWIM**          **FINS**

**WAVES**          **FISH**          **TIDE**

**SALTWATER**          **FRESHWATER**          **SURF**

Answers on page 69

41

# FEEL THE FEAR

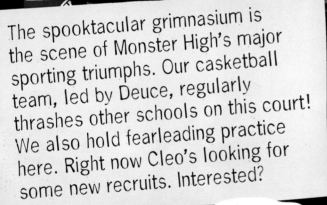

The spooktacular grimnasium is the scene of Monster High's major sporting triumphs. Our casketball team, led by Deuce, regularly thrashes other schools on this court! We also hold fearleading practice here. Right now Cleo's looking for some new recruits. Interested?

If you want to impress Cleo, you'll need to pull out all of the stops! There are eight scary-cool frames on this page. Use them to plot out your very own monster cheer routine! Think up a clawsome set of steps, then draw one move into each panel. Good luck!

# POSTER GHOULS

OK, your cheer was not totally dreadful. I might just give you a place on the fear squad if you can draw a poster for our upcoming fearleading competition. It's taking place in the grimnasium, on Halloween, at midnight. Make sure it looks totally golden!

Pick out your favorite pens and start designing! Cleo's team needs a poster that will get Monster High's fearleading fans flocking to the grim—think fierce, fly, and freaky on the eye. Oh. My. Ra!

# CLEO'S COLOR COPY

This is my favorite picture of the fearleading squad after the trials for Monster Mashionals! Help Ghoulia get it copied and posted up all over the school so that everyone knows how totally creeperific we are.

Are you ready to start drawing? The best way to get your picture eek-xactly right is to copy each square into the blank one on this page. When you've finished drawing, color in the picture.

# CLEO'S RA-CIPES

Eeeugh! Never in my 5,843 years have I tasted anything as disgusting as the slimy slop served up in the creepateria! I'm campaigning to have the menu changed to suit my—I mean, everybody's—tastes. These Ra-cipes have been passed down through my family over the millennia.

Try cooking up a creepy cauldron

## Creeperific Cucumber Dip

*This is ugh-mazing served with toasted pita bread!*—Frankie Stein

### You will need:

1 small cucumber
Pinch of salt
Handful of mint leaves
1 clove garlic, finely chopped (optional)
16oz container plain Greek yogurt
Drizzle of olive oil

### Here's what you do:

1. Slice the cucumber lengthwise and carefully remove the seeds with a teaspoon.

2. Finely dice the cucumber into tiny chunks.

3. Place the cucumber into a shallow bowl and sprinkle with a pinch of salt. Leave for an hour until all the liquid has been drawn out of the cucumber.

4. While the liquid is draining from the cucumber, finely chop the mint leaves and the garlic. (Some monsters, especially vampires, don't like garlic, so you can leave it out.)

5. Drain the liquid away from the cucumber and combine the cucumber in a clean bowl with the yogurt, garlic, mint, and a drizzle of olive oil.

6. Chill the dip in the fridge before serving to your best ghoulfriends!

# Deadly Delicious Dessert

his frozen feast based on Khoshaf
sauce so yummy it would sweeten yeti!
—Abbey Bominable

## For at least four servings, you will need:

½ cup orange juice
1 ¼ cup water
½ cup sugar
1 cup chopped dried apricots
¾ cup golden raisins
¾ cup raisins
16oz container vanilla ice cream

## Here's what you do:

1. Bring the orange juice, water, and sugar to a boil in a small saucepan, stirring the mixture frequently.

2. Add the dried fruits, then bring the mixture to a boil again.

3. Simmer the fruits for 10 minutes before carefully removing from the heat. Allow the pan to cool slightly.

4. Place one or two scoops of ice cream in four small serving bowls.

5. Drizzle the warm fruity sauce over the top of each bowl. Freaktacular!

# Scary-cool Fruit Snack

Eat these naturally sweet
dates straight from the fridge,
or try this twist for a glam
party snack.
—Nefera de Nile

## You will need:

8oz package of Medjool dates
4oz milk chocolate
Dusting of confectioners' sugar

## Here's what you do:

1. Break the chocolate into squares and place the pieces in a heatproof bowl. Suspend the bowl over a pan of simmering water, but do not allow the bottom to touch the water.

2. Heat the chocolate, stirring regularly, until it's almost completely melted, then remove it from the heat.

3. Dip one end of each date in the melted chocolate, then place it on a plate. Keep going until every date has been dipped. Put the dates in the fridge.

4. When the chocolate has set, sprinkle the dates with confectioners' sugar. Serve them to your GFFs and wait for the screams of delight!

# The Monster High-clopedia

In the libury there are many ancient books, including the Monster High-clopedia, which details the many lessons the student bodies have learned as they pass through the school. Here are two such tales . . .

## TOUGH AS SCALES

One day in metalwork class . . .

Killer job on the stand, Jinafire

The fire-breathing daughter of the Chinese Dragon had welded a mount for the winning casketball.

*This ball's irreplaceable!*

*Careful, Flame-brain!*

But while the guys were arguing . . .

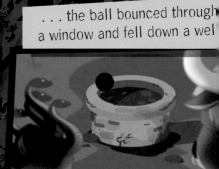

. . . the ball bounced through a window and fell down a well

Jinafire led the boys underground to find it.

*Step aside. Let Manny show ya how it's done!*

The boys were sure they could reach the ball.

*We need to calculate the distance down and then . . .*

... melt the bars!

Owww!

Problems aren't always solved with demonstrations of strength!

Jinafire told them about her childhood . . .

One day her father sent his children to capture a beast that was terrorizing the village.

Her brothers tried to bring the beast out with force and aggression . . .

. . . but the only thing they returned with were broken bones.

Back at Monster High . . .

Jinafire blew on her hair ornament and threw it at a stalactite. It fell, damming the stream.

Jinafire was wiser. Rather than try to force her way in . . .

. . . her fire forced the beast out of its cave into a cage.

The ball floated back up, proving Jinafire's point, but a monster floated up with it!

I think I should hold on to the ball!

Jinafire used fire to blast the monster back down. Even she had to admit that force did sometimes help!

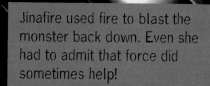

THE END

49

# Th Monste. High-clopedia

Here's another tale from The Monster High-clopedia. It shows the important lesson a new student taught us about never judging a book by its cover!

# Ready, Wheeling, and Able

The ghouls were discussing the new monster in school.

What's this ne kid's name?

Rider—bet he's a natural athlete!

Clawd would break a leash to get another guy for Skultimate Rollermaze!

Suddenly something came flying round a corner . . .

Oh man! This place is spin-credible!

From the look of his blog, this kid's pretty intense!

Oh hi! Monster High is totally a place where you can be yourself!

What're we gonna check out first?

Maybe we shouldn't show him . . . all the sports stuff.

Penmanship class?

Awesome, right?!

What if he got hurt?

The worried ghouls took Rider somewhere safe . . .

We've got some voltageous activities planned.

Libury Club, Wool Collecting Club, Rock and Pebble Society . . .

This is what you guys do for fun?

I heard so much spook-takular stuff about Monster High, but none of it's true!

Frankie ran Rider through the most boring clubs at Monster High.

I may have told him that Scream is the most epic thing you can possibly do!

Whooooo-hoooo!

The gnom.... looked for Rider.....

Then Toralei slyly admitted she'd directed Rider toward the scream track.

Sure enough, Rider was burning rubber in the grim.

How could you let him on the scream track? It's not safe!

Maybe he knows better than us what he can and can't do!

Draculaura rounded on Clawd.

Suddenly there was a crash!

This is who I am. If I need help, I'll ask. Cool?

I dunno . . .

Yeah.

THE END

That was totally spin-sane!!! I'm going again!

Rider reminded Frankie that she'd said he could be himself at Monster High.

Will you light my wheels on fire? I wanna try this again!

# THROW A DAY OF THE DEAD PARTY

*Hola!* I'm so excited that Headmistress Bloodgood is going to allow us to use the Great Howl for a Day of the Dead party this year. It is going to be so much fun! I cannot wait to introduce all the ghouls to my creeptastic culture.

The Day of the Dead is a holiday celebrated all across the world. On November 1 and 2, ghouls get together to remember fiends and family that have passed away. There are all kinds of parties and traditions. If you can't make it to Monster High this year, why not use Skelita's tips to skelebrate with your boos?

Even party ghouls need to be safe! Ask an adult before using scissors, skewers, or sharp knives.

## PAPER MARIGOLDS

### YOU WILL NEED:

- Thin tissue paper in bright shades of yellow and orange
- Ruler
- Scissors
- Pipe cleaners or pieces of ribbon (one for each flower)

### HERE'S WHAT YOU DO:

1. Layer five sheets of tissue paper on top of one another to make a pile. Trim them with scissors to create a 1 ½ x 6 inch rectangle.

2. Starting at the shorter end at the bottom, fold up 1 inch of the stacked paper to begin making a fan.

3. Continue folding the paper until you reach the top.

4. Pinch the center of the fan together, then tie it with a pipe cleaner or piece of ribbon.

5. Gently pull apart each layer of the fan until all the tissue forms the petals of a flower.

1 box of cupcake mix
White ready-mixed buttercream frosting
Black icing pen

- Brightly colored candies
- Blue or pink icing pens (optional)
- Sugar sprinkles

## HERE'S WHAT YOU DO:

1. Bake the cupcakes according to the instructions on the box. Don't forget to ask your creator before using the oven.

2. When the cupcakes are cooked and cooled, scarefully ice each one with a thin covering of white buttercream frosting.

3. Draw a skeleton mouth on each cupcake using the black icing pen. Outline a thin smile with little black "stitches" going across it like a railroad.

4. Now you can really get creative! Use candies or icing pens to make the eyes, then top the outer edge of each cupcake with sugar sprinkles.

5. If you have room you could also use the icing pens to add extra flourishes to your cupcakes, such as swirly lines or flowers.

These cupcakes don't just taste good. They also make a great party centerpiece!

## YOU WILL NEED:

Pencil
White card
Scissors

- Coloring pens or pencils
- A skewer or sharp knife
- Piece of elastic

## HERE'S WHAT YOU DO:

Draw a larger version of the Monster High Skullette onto a sheet of white card.

Cut out both of the eye holes.

Decorate the mask with beautiful flower designs in colored pens or pencils. Use yellows, blues, greens, pinks, and oranges.

These masks are a real Day of the Dead tradition in Mexico! If you don't want to make masks, you can use face-paints.

4. Scarefully make a small hole at ear level on each side of the Skullette with a skewer or sharp knife. Thread a piece of elastic through the back and tie it in place!

# Fierce Green Fashion

Venus has got me thinking about how monsters have an impact on the environment. We've come up with some upcycling ideas to help ghouls look fierce while helping to protect the planet. We're displaying our creeptastic green collection in the school's Great Howl. Take a look!

Don't throw away your old clothes! Let Venus and Clawdeen inspire you instead. These scarylicious upcycling projects can all be made from a few old T-shirts.

## You will need:

- Scissors
- Cardboard
- Some old T-shirts
- Large beads
- Photo frame

## Scary-cute Crop Top

### Here's what you do:

1. Cut the sleeves and neck off the T-shirt.

2. Cut the T-shirt into a cropped top, leaving two long strips of material at the front.

3. Tug on the edges to make them look less freshly cut, then pull on the two strips so that they become more stringlike.

4. Knot the two stringy strips together to create a cute tied detail.

5. Wear your crop top over a longer tank top in a contrasting color. Totally voltage!

# Freaky-Funky Fringe Tank

Check with an adult before using scissors. Make sure it's OK before snipping a chunk out of any of your old clothes!

## Here's what you do:

1. Cut the sleeves and neck off the T-shirt.

2. Starting at the front of the tee, cut vertically upward from the hem to about a third of the way up. Repeat across the front so that the bottom hangs in a fringe of strings.

3. Pull on the strings to thin them out, then repeat the cuts along the back of the T-shirt.

4. Take a string and thread a colored bead on to it. Tie a knot at the end to hold the bead in place.

5. Work your way all around the T-shirt, beading and knotting each string. You'll end up with a freaktacular beaded fringe that swishes as you move.

# Nostalgic Tee Picture

## Here's what you do:

1. Do you have a favorite T-shirt that's too small to wear any more? If you still love the picture on the front, cut it out!

2. Wrap the cut-out fabric around a piece of cardboard, with the picture on the front. Then use tape or glue to secure the fabric at the back.

3. Fit the cardboard into a photo frame to turn your old T-shirt into a piece of ugh-mazing art!

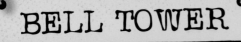
Rochelle and I can both be found floating around the bell tower. I monster-watch from up here, looking for inspiration for my column. Rochelle just feels most at home when she's near (or on) the roof.

How well do you know Monster High's bell-tower beauties? Underline the words that sum up Rochelle in gray and those that make you think of Spectra in purple.

Rock Candy

Violet

Protective

Griffin

Silk

Angel Cake

Pale

Rhuen

Persistent

Transparent

Floating

Disgruntled

Chains

Roux

Scaris

Kind

Haunting

Defensive

Ferret

Curious

Iron

Stained Glass

Journalism

Architecture

Pigeons

Sculpting

Rattle

Ghostly Gossip

Grey

Spectra and Rochelle have a ghoul's-eye view of comings and groanings at Monster High. What do you think they've just spotted? Draw the scene here!

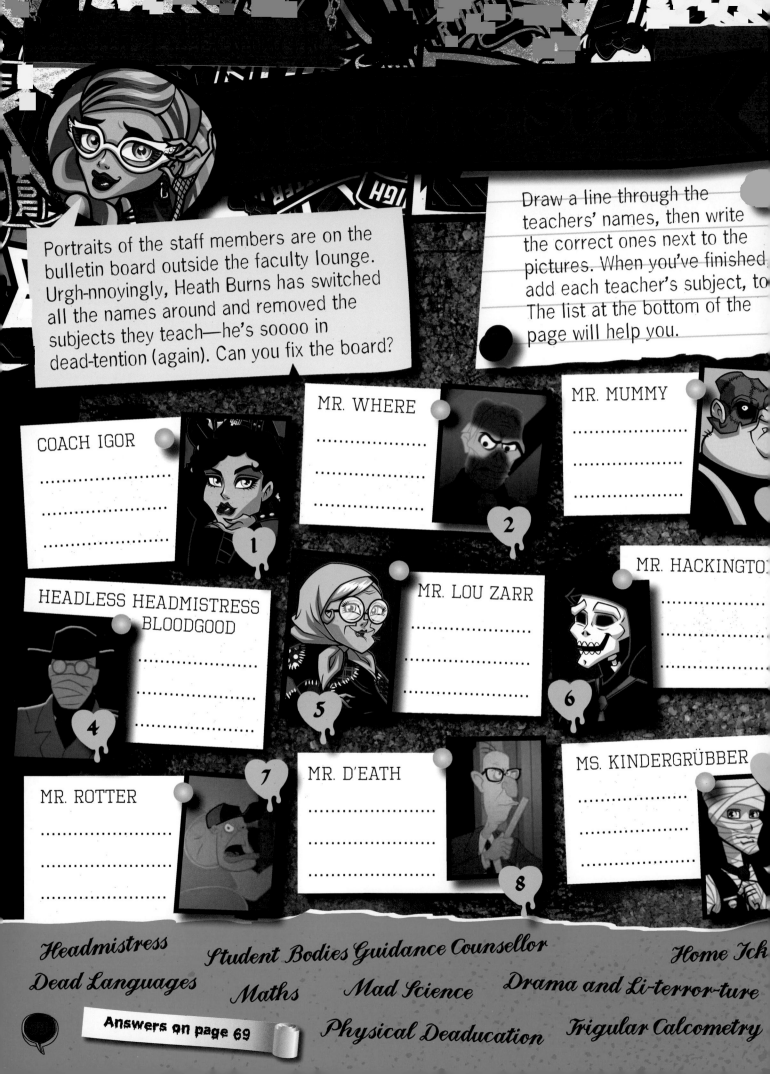

Portraits of the staff members are on the bulletin board outside the faculty lounge. Urgh-nnoyingly, Heath Burns has switched all the names around and removed the subjects they teach—he's soooo in dead-tention (again). Can you fix the board?

Draw a line through the teachers' names, then write the correct ones next to the pictures. When you've finished, add each teacher's subject, too. The list at the bottom of the page will help you.

COACH IGOR
..................
..................
..................
1

MR. WHERE
..................
..................
..................
2

MR. MUMMY
..................
..................

HEADLESS HEADMISTRESS BLOODGOOD
..................
..................
..................
4

MR. LOU ZARR
..................
..................
..................
5

MR. HACKINGTO...
..................
..................
6

MR. ROTTER
..................
..................
..................

MR. D'EATH
..................
..................
..................
7

MS. KINDERGRÜBBER
..................
..................
..................
8

*Headmistress*        *Student Bodies*  *Guidance Counsellor*                *Home Ick...*

*Dead Languages*          *Maths*        *Mad Science*     *Drama and Li-terror-ture*

**Answers on page 69**     *Physical Deaducation*      *Trigular Calcometry*

Now that you have had time to look around the school, let's see how well you know my monstrously academic staff members. The answers are on page 69, but cheating will result in a spell in the Pit of Horror . . .

**1.** Complete Mr. Mummy's favorite quote:

"Knowledge is the _ _ _ _
for every curse."

**2.** Mr. D'eath has a habit of constantly sighing and keeps a "regret list" about the things he wishes he hadn't done. True or false?

..............................................

**3.** Which teacher has a degree in Candy Construction?

..............................................

**4.** "To see or not to be seen—that is the question,'" is the favorite quote of which teacher?

..............................................

**5.** What is Mr. Hackington more commonly known as among the student bodies?

..............................................

**6.** Which faculty does Mr. Mummy head up?

..............................................

**7.** S.A.T.s are the regular examinations set by the staff of Monster High. What do the letters stand for?

..............................................

**8.** Which unfortunately named creature is actually a substitute creature, rather than a permanent member of staff?
A. Mr. Mummy ☐
B. Mr. D'eath ☐
C. Mr. Lou Zarr ☐

**9.** In Home Ick, what skill does Ms. Kindergrübber teach aside from cooking?

..............................................

**10.** Which teacher once entrusted his students with looking after a gargoyle egg?

..............................................

# BEACHY KEEN

Gloom Beach is one of my favorite places in the world. Spending all day swimming in the ocean and all night in a dorm with my beast ghoulfriends—bliss! I was stoked to get hold of this great photo of us at Gloom Beach. I've made copies for all my GFFs!

A

B

C

D

One of Lagoona's prints is not quite the same as the other three. Can you spot the odd photo out?

# Gloom-y Ghouls

It's another horrifically hot day at Gloom Beach and after playing water polo with Gil all afternoon, I just want to relax on a lounge chair with me mates. Trouble is, the vampires from Smogsnorts Academy have taken most of the lounge chairs!

Which ghouls will be able to sit down and which ones will be left on the sand? Follow the trails of sun scream to find out.

Answers on page 69

# Ghostcard From
# SCARIS

Rochelle's ghostcard has been written on a stone tablet, but it's been monster-handled in the mail! Some of the vowels have chipped off. Can you fill in the gaps so that Rochelle can hear the news from Scaris?

Oh, I am sooo 'appy! I 'ave receive a ghostcard from 'ome. I adore being at Monster 'igh, but sometime I cannot 'elp missing ze city and ze buildings where I grew up. If only I could read it!

BY AIR MAIL
PAR AVION

I _ar R_ch_ll_,

Gr___tings fr_m Scar_s!

_ll the G_rgoyl_s send th___r l_ve.
_e m_ss s____ng y__r st_ny gaz_ _cross
th_ r_oft_ps.

L_st week was f_shi_n week _nd Moanat_lla
Gh_stier st_ged her sh_w in the crypts _f
Ogre Dame Cath_dral. It w_s pr_tty
sp__ktacul_r b_t n_t as ugh-m_zing as
Garrott du Roqu_'s. Your fr_end is r_ally
making a spl_sh w_th his l_test c_llection!

H_pe all's fr_aky-f_bul_us with you.

L_ve M_m & D_d xx

Answers on page 69

# What's in Store?

I just love the maul. Shopping is my favorite activity—being fur-rociously stylish, I love to spend my time checking out the fierce fashions in-store. I know every outlet like the back of my paw. What about you?

Do you know Clawdeen's favorite haunts? Unscramble the letters to reveal the most fabulous stores in the maul. The correct names are mixed up at the bottom of the page to give you a clue.

MAVL

**A** HET FFICNO ABEN

_ _ _ _ _ _ _ _ _ _ _

**F** RANSLVANTYIA'S TECSCRE

_ _ _ _ _ _ _ _ _ _ _ , _ _ _ _ _ _ _ _

**B** RREBUFRY

_ _ _ _ _ _ _ _

**E** STRIEHOG

_ _ _ _ _ _ _ _

**G** KRAB BACOMS

_ _ _ _ _ _ _ _ _ _

**C** ACELOUGH

_ _ _ _ _ _ _ _

**D** HET DOOF TWALC

_ _ _ _ _ _ _ _ _ _ _

**H** IED-ERN

_ _ _ _ _ _ _

TRANSYLVANIA'S SECRET

THE COFFIN BEAN

DIE-NER

BARK MACOBS

FURBERR

THE BOOT CLAWT

CHOCLAC

GHOSTER

Answers on page 69

They always have amazing films playing on the big scream in the maul's movie theater. It's positively electrifying! It's where I took Frankie for our first—and last—date. I love watching horro-mantic comedies, but most of the monsters prefer to freak out at scary human movies.

Use this page to create a plot for your own Monster High movie. Maybe you'll have Ghoulia ousting Cleo from the fear squad or show Jackson finally getting the ghoul . . .

# COLOR US CREEPY

I'm ghosting a creepover tonight, but before we get some sleep in my superking-sized coffin, I'm giving my GFFs makeovers in my powder room. Want to help? Make each ghoul look gore-geous!

Use your pens and pencils to give each ghoul a fangtastic new look.

# Screams of Squares

**You will need:**

- 2 players
- A pen or pencil per player

Cleo is insisting that we play her favorite creepover game, Gargoyles to Gargoyles, but I'm putting my paw down. We always play that and she goes totally cryptic every time she loses! I'm suggesting my fabulous squares game instead. Want to play?

## Rules:

- The goal of the game is to "own" as many squares as possible. The squares that you own will be those with your initial inside them.

- The youngest player goes first, joining two dots with a line. Play then passes to the next player, who draws another line. Each new line must connect with a line that's already on the board.

- Players continue to take turns until someone draws a line that completes a square shape. Any player completing a square should write their initial in the center and take another turn. (You can just write over the Skullette if there's one in the square). The game continues until all the squares are complete.

- The winner is the player with the most points! Score 1 point for every square containing your initial. Score 3 points for every square containing your initial and a Skullette.

LATER, GHOULFRIEND!

## ANSWERS

### PAGES 22-23:
### MY SPOOKY SCARE-ITAGE

**Name:** Skelita *Calaveras*
**Dead-scended from:** Los Eskeletos
**Scary-cool country:** Hexico
**My scare-itage:** I am very proud of my scare-itage and its legends and traditions. My favorite custom is *Dia de los* Muertos or Day of the Dead, where we honor our ancestors. We spend time with *la familia*, hold parties, and decorate our homes with marigold flowers and screamily scrummy sugar skulls.

**Name:** Jinafire Long
**Dead-scended from:** Chinese Dragons
**Scary-cool country:** China
**My scare-itage:** The country of my fore-monsters is very eek-xotic, with customs and traditions that have carried on for thousands and thousands of years. Monsters like me were often found guarding temples. We have always had great powers and can control elements including fire, wind, and water.

**Name:** Cleo de Nile
**Dead-scended from:** The Mummy
**Scary-cool country:** Egypt
**My scare-itage:** My father tells me that traditionally monsters like me were entombed in pyramids in the middle of the desert with jewels and gold and sooo much bling. We still live in my father's pyramid and I have my own, totes amazing crypt! Our bodies were wrapped in an OTT amount of bandages—the updated version of this look we now call "body-con."

**Name:** Rochelle Goyle
**Dead-scended from:** The Gargoyles
**Scary-cool city:** Scaris
**My scare-itage:** Stone is a big part of my culture. My ancestors have always been found on and around great buildings such as castles and cathedrals, which we protect. Although I come from Scaris, monsters like me are found in many countries, including ancient Egypt and Greece. We can take many forms.

### PAGE 25:
### LI-TERROR-TURE

1. HOLT HYDE
2. FRANKIE STEIN
3. VENUS MCFLYTRAP
4. CLAWD WOLF

# PAGES 28-29:
## SPA QUIZ

1. B
2. Casketball
3. HOME ICK
4. All of them—Frankie's currents cause problems in the water, Rochelle sinks like a stone, and there is a large octo-creature lurking in the caves beneath the pool!
5. Mr. Hackington
6. Mr. Rotter
7. The catacombs
8. In their coffin lockers
9. True (although Lagoona sometimes smuggles in Neptuna, her pet piranha, in her water-filled bag)
10. Nightmare
11. C
12. A
13. They are all extra-scare-icular activities at Monster High

# PAGE 32:
## COUNSELING CONUNDRUM

1. B
2. C
3. D
4. A

# PAGE 33:
## ZOMBIE SUPERHIGHWAY

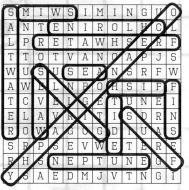

START

FINISH

# PAGE 34:
## HEADS WILL ROLL!

1–D, 2–C, 3–E, 4–A, 5–B

# PAGE 35:
## HOO'S HOO IN THE 'COMBS?

1. Abbey Bominable
2. Jinafire Long
3. Toralei Stripe
4. Clawd Wolf
5. Skelita Calaveras
6. Venus McFlytrap
7. HooDude Voodoo
8. Draculaura

# PAGE 41:
## LAGOONA'S WATERY WORDSEARCH

The extra word is CHLORINE.

| S | M | I | W | S | I | M | I | N | G | U | O |
|---|---|---|---|---|---|---|---|---|---|---|---|
| A | N | T | E | N | I | R | O | L | H | C | L |
| L | P | R | E | T | A | W | H | S | E | R | F |
| T | O | T | V | A | N | Q | A | P | J | S | A |
| W | U | S | U | S | E | A | N | S | R | F | W |
| A | W | E | L | N | F | O | H | S | I | F | F |
| T | C | V | E | G | E | T | U | N | E | I | I |
| E | L | A | V | A | T | I | S | D | R | N | N |
| R | O | W | A | G | U | G | D | I | U | A | S |
| S | R | P | S | E | V | W | E | T | E | R | F |
| R | H | S | N | E | P | T | U | N | E | G | F |
| Y | S | A | E | D | M | J | V | T | N | G | I |

# PAGES 56-57:
## BELL-TOWER BEAUTIES

### Spectra's words:
Violet, Angel Cake, Curious, Persistent, Floating, Transparent, Ghostly Gossip, Journalism, Haunting, Chains, Pale, Kind, Rhuen, Rattle, Silk, Defensive, Ferret.

### Rochelle's words:
Rock Candy, Iron, Stained Glass, Griffin, Protective, Architecture, Gray, Sculpting, Roux, Scaris, Pigeons, Disgruntled.

# PAGE 58:
## MEET THE STAFF

1. Headless Headmistress Bloodgood
   HEADMISTRESS
2. Mr. Rotter
   DEAD LANGUAGES
3. Mr. Hackington
   MAD SCIENCE
4. Mr. Where
   DRAMA AND LI-TERROR-TURE
5. Ms. Kindergrübber
   HOME ICK
6. Mr. D'eath
   STUDENT BODIES
   GUIDANCE COUNSELOR
7. Coach Igor
   PHYSICAL DEADUCATION
8. Mr. Lou Zarr
   TRIGULAR CALCOMETRY
9. Mr. Mummy
   MATH

# PAGE 59:
## CREATURE TEACHER QUIZ

1. "Knowledge is the cure for every curse."
2. True
3. Ms. Kindergrübber
4. Mr. Where
5. Mr. Hack
6. Math
7. Scary Aptitude Tests
8. Mr. Lou Zarr ('Mr. Loser', get it?!)
9. Sewing
10. Mr. Hackington

# PAGE 60:
## BEACHY KEEN

B.

# PAGE 61:
## GLOOM-Y GHOULS

Only Ghoulia and Draculaura will get to sit on the lounge chairs.

# PAGE 62:
## GHOSTCARD FROM SCARIS

Dear Rochelle,
Greetings from Scaris!
All the Gargoyles send their love.
We miss seeing your stony gaze across the rooftops. Last week was Fashion Week and Moanatella Ghostier staged her show in the crypts of Ogre Dame Cathedral. It was pretty spooktacular but not as ugh-mazing as Garrott du Roque's. Your friend is really making a splash with this latest collection!
Hope all's freaky-fabulous with you.
Love, Mom & Dad xxx

# PAGE 64:
## WHAT'S IN STORE?

A. THE COFFIN BEAN
B. FURBERRY
C. GHOULACE
D. THE FOOD CLAWT
E. GHOSTIER
F. TRANSYLVANIA'S SECRET
G. BARK MACOBS
H. DIE-NER

MONSTER HIGH

69